This Bing book belongs to:

. . . .

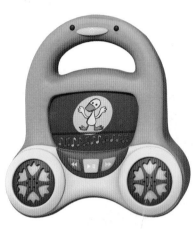

Copyright © 2019 Acamar Films Ltd

The Bing television series is created by Acamar Films and Brown Bag Films
and adapted from the original books by Ted Dewan

Based on the episode *Birthday* by Lead Writer An Vrombaut and Team Writers Mikael Shields and Claire Jennings

Written by Rebecca Gerlings
Images by Shadid Omar
Designed by Candice Turvey
Edited by Annabel Walwyn and Freddie Hutchins

First published in the UK in 2019 by HarperCollins *Children's Books*
A division of HarperCollins *Publishers* Ltd, 1 London Bridge Street, London, SE1 9GF

10 9 8 7 6 5 4 3 2 1

ISBN: 978-0-00-832615-9

Printed in China

Bing's Birthday Party!

HarperCollins *Children's Books*

Round the corner, not far away,
Bing is having a **birthday** today.

Bing and Flop are in the kitchen, getting ready for Bing's birthday party.

"Look, Flop. My pass the parcel is getting bigger and bigger and bigger!"

"Indeed," says Flop.

"Happy birthday, Bing!"

Sula spots Bing's new toy. "What's that, Bing?" she asks.

"It's my Waka-oke machine. I got it for my birthday," Bing says, proudly.

He clips on the
special microphone,
ready to show them
how it works.

"Watch!" says Bing, tapping the screen.

Tap!

The Waka-oke duck appears. **"Let's do the Waka-oke!"** it says.

"Waka-waka-waka-waka-waka-waka-oke!" sings the duck. Bing quacks his hands along to the music.

"WOW!" Sula, Pando and Coco watch Bing, laughing.

"Flapa-flapa-flapa-flapa-flapa-flapa-oke!" Bing sings, flapping his arms.

"Pada-pada-pada-pada-pada-pada-oke!" sing the duck and Bing together, stamping their feet up and down.

The Waka-oke
looks like so
much fun.
Bing's friends
can't wait
to have a go!

"My turn first!"
shouts Pando.

Coco reminds him that Bing can choose who goes first because it's his birthday.

Bing thinks. "Er, Sula can go first," he says. "Then you, Pando. And then you, Coco."

Tap!

"Waka-waka-waka-waka-waka-waka-oke!" sings the duck again.

But Sula gets it wrong! She flapa-flapa-flaps instead.

Bing explains that she has to do the **waka-waka** first and shows Sula how to do it.

"Oh, yes!" says Sula, remembering.

Then Sula **flapa-flaps** so well that the microphone falls off her dress. Whoops!

"My turn now!" shouts Pando, grabbing it.

Tap!

"Flapa-waka-flapa-waka-flapa-waka-oke!" sings Pando, quacking and flapping and stamping all at once.

That's not right...
Pando isn't doing it properly!

"Why don't you show Pando how to do it, Bing?" suggests Flop. "Then you can both play." Flop goes into the kitchen to find the candles for Bing's birthday cake.

"Can you show me and Coco how
to do it too, Bing?" asks Sula.

"OK," agrees Bing, "but you all
have to stand in a line."

Tap!

But Pando is too excited to stand in line . . .

Waka-waka-waka-waka-
waka-waka-oke!

"No, Pando!" cries Bing. "You're doing
it all wrong again! Stop it!"

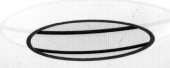

But Pando doesn't listen.

Flapa-flapa-flapa-flapa-
flapa-flapa-oke!

Bing can't wait for his party to start. His friends Sula, Pando, Coco, Charlie and Amma have all been invited.

"First, we're going to play pass the parcel, then we're going to play the Waka-oke!" Bing tells Flop. "And then, we're going to eat my cake!"

DING DONG!

Bing rushes to the front door.

Everybody's here! And they've brought prese

Pando, Sula and Coco all dance, and dance, and dance!

Pada-pada-pada-pada-pada-pada-oke!

"I love the Waka-oke machine!" shouts Pando, spinning about.

Bing wants
Pando to stop.
He runs into the
kitchen to find Flop.

"Flop!" he calls over
the Waka-oke music.
But Flop isn't there.
"Oh, Flop . . ."
whispers Bing.
"Where are you?"

The Waka-oke music stops.

"Oh!" says Sula.
"Where's Bing?"

"Hmmm, I don't know,
Sula," replies Flop,
coming out from the
cupboard. "I think I'll
have a look upstairs . . ."

Flop goes into Bing's bedroom. Oh – what's that under the duvet?

"Bing... Are you in there?"

Bing doesn't reply.

"Are you feeling a bit under-the-blankety?"

"Yup..."

"What happened, Bing?" asks Flop.

"It's not my birthday party any more," says Bing, sadly. "Pando did the Waka-oke all wrong, and he wouldn't stop. And he did too much loud singing."

"Yes, well, Pando does like singing," says Flop.

"And then... I couldn't find you, Flop," sniffs Bing.

"Well, I'm here now," replies Flop, gently. "Are you feeling a bit better?"

"Yup..."

KNOCK
KNOCK
KNOCK

"Can we come in?" asks Sula,
peeping under Bing's blanket.

"Yup," says Bing, quietly.

Next, Pando's face appears. "Happy birthday,
Bing!" he says, giving Bing his present.

"Oh, thank you!" Bing says, happy to see his friends again.

Now everyone is under the blanket!

"Flop!" Bing says, laughing. "I'm having a different happy birthday!"

"Indeed," agrees Flop.

After a game of pass the parcel, it's time for Bing's birthday cake.

"Happy birthday, Bing!"

his friends shout.

Bing takes a big breath and blows out all his candles.

"Good for you, Bing Bunny!" says Flop, smiling.

Birthdays . . . they're a Bing thing.